THE GLORIOUS MOTHER GOOSE

Fanny Cory, 1913

THE GLORIOUS MOTHER GOOSE

SELECTED BY

COOPER EDENS

WITH ILLUSTRATIONS BY
THE BEST ARTISTS FROM THE PAST

Atheneum Books for Young Readers

Atheneum Books for Young Readers
An imprint of Simon & Schuster Children's Publishing Division
1230 Avenue of the Americas
New York, New York 10020

Printed in United States of America
First Atheneum Books for Young Readers Edition, 1988
Revised Jacket Edition, 1998

10   9   8   7   6   5   4   3   2   1

Library of Congress Cataloging-in-Publication Data
Mother Goose. Selections.
The glorious Mother Goose : selections by Cooper Edens.—rev. jacket ed.
p.   cm.
Summary: A collection of nursery rhymes, including those about Humpty Dumpty,
Jack and Jill, Little Jack Horner, and Little Miss Muffet.
1. Nursery rhymes. 2. Children's poetry. [1. Nursery rhymes.]
I. Edens, Cooper. II. Title.
PZ8.3.M85   1998
398'.8—dc21   97-38444

ISBN 0-689-82050-X

THE DATE GIVEN FOR EACH ILLUSTRATION IS THE DATE OF THE
ILLUSTRATION'S FIRST PUBLICATION.

FIRST
EDITION

CONTENTS

(in alphabetical order by first line)

E. Boyd Smith, 1919

Foreword

The true identity of Mother Goose, if any, may never be determined, but perhaps that is for the best. Somehow, knowing would diminish the charm of the character in our imaginations and detract from the joy of reading and saying aloud the rhymes that have survived so many childhoods. There is mystery and magic in Mother Goose's unflagging popularity across generations and life-styles. The source and meaning of each rhyme is, after all, unimportant. What is important is that the ones that remain are guaranteed to be the favorites of generations to come.

Over the years I have turned the pages of dozens of illustrated collections of Mother Goose rhymes and have enjoyed again and again the music in the words and the wonderful images they evoke. We are free to make of them what we will, and generations of artists have exulted in that same freedom. For this volume, I have chosen, for the most part, the more familiar rhymes. To accompany them I have selected my favorite illustrations from the many hundreds I have seen, both in color and in black and white. I think you will be fascinated to see the divergent interpretations offered by the various illustrators. One artist, for example, depicts Mary, Mary Quite Contrary as a little girl, another as a grown woman. Little Jack Horner is the sweetest of boys to one, and a rascal to another. *The Glorious Mother Goose*, however, is not intended as a scholarly survey of the history of children's book illustrators. It is simply meant to offer readers a rich diversity of styles and moods created by artists who, themselves, are as varied as the rhymes and the children who have loved them. I like to think that Mother Goose would be pleased with this evidence of her bountiful heritage—whoever she may have been.

C. E.

February 1988

NIGHT SQUALLS

H. L. Stephens, 1884

⌒ THE ⌒
GLORIOUS
MOTHER
GOOSE

Baa, baa, Black Sheep,
Have you any wool?
Yes, marry, have I,
Three bags full:

One for my master,
And one for my dame,
And one for the little boy
That lives in the lane!

Curly locks! Curly locks! Wilt thou be mine?
Thou shalt not wash dishes, nor yet feed the swine;
But sit on a cushion and sew a fine seam,
And feed upon strawberries, sugar, and cream!

Goosey, goosey, gander, where shall I wander?
Up stairs, down stairs, and in my lady's chamber;
There I met an old man that would not say his prayers;
I took him by the left leg, and threw him down stairs.

Here we go round the mulberry bush,
The mulberry bush, the mulberry bush,
Here we go round the mulberry bush,
On a cold and frosty morning.

Hey, diddle, diddle, the cat and the fiddle,
The cow jumped over the moon;
The little dog laughed to see such sport,
While the dish ran away with the spoon.

Hickory, dickory, dock,
The mouse ran up the clock,
The clock struck one,
The mouse ran down,
Hickory, dickory, dock.

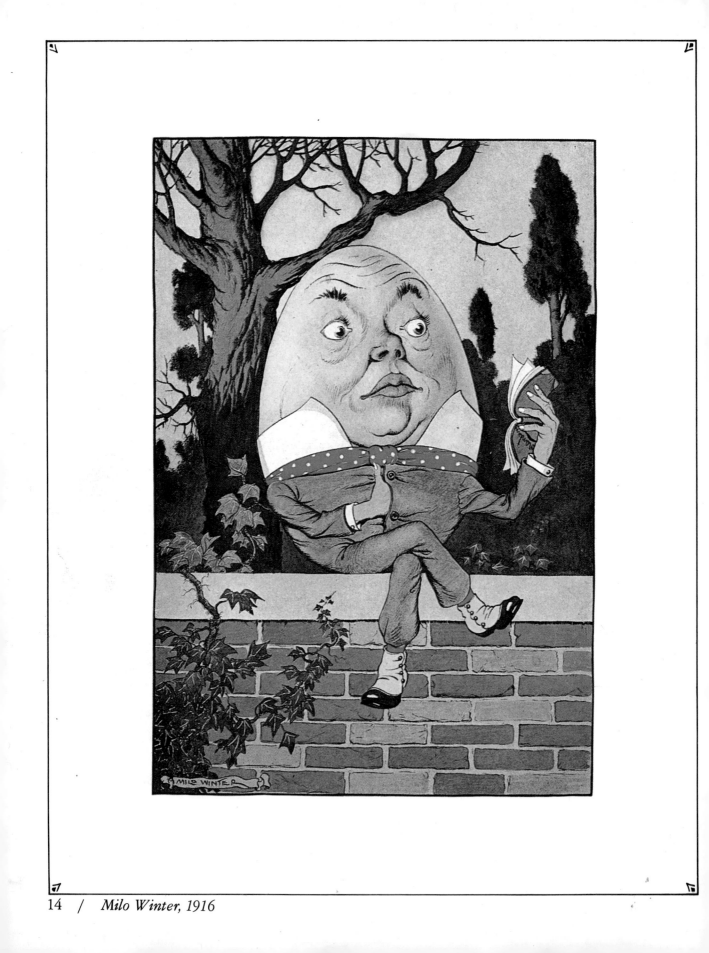

Humpty Dumpty sat on a wall,
Humpty Dumpty had a great fall;
All the king's horses and all the king's men
Couldn't put Humpty together again.

Hush-a-bye, baby, on the tree top,
When the wind blows the cradle will rock;
When the bough breaks the cradle will fall,
And down comes baby and cradle and all.

I had a little nut tree; nothing would it bear
But a silver nutmeg and a golden pear;
The king of Spain's daughter came to visit me,
And all was because of my little nut tree.
I skipped over water, I danced over sea,
And all the birds in the air couldn't catch me.

Jack and Jill
Went up the hill,
To fetch a pail of water;
Jack fell down,
And broke his crown,
And Jill came tumbling after.

Jack be nimble, Jack be quick,
Jack jump over the candlestick.

Jack Sprat could eat no fat
His wife could eat no lean;
And so betwixt them both,
They licked the platter clean.

Little Bo-peep has lost her sheep,
And can't tell where to find them;
Leave them alone, and they'll come home,
And bring their tails behind them.

Little Boy Blue, come blow your horn,
The sheep's in the meadow, the cow's in the corn.
Where is the boy who looks after the sheep?
He's under a haycock fast asleep.
Will you wake him? No, not I,
For if I do, he's sure to cry.

Little Jack Horner
Sat in a corner,
Eating a Christmas pie;
He put in his thumb,
And pulled out a plum,
And cried: "What a good boy am I!"

COPYRIGHT 1901.
BY NOYES, PLATT & COMPANY.

Peter Newell

Little Miss Muffet
Sat on a tuffet,
Eating her curds and whey;
When down came a spider,
And sat down beside her,
And frightened Miss Muffet away.

Little Tom Tucker, sing for your supper.
What shall he sing for? White bread and butter.
How shall he cut it without any knife?
How shall he marry without any wife?

36 / *Jennie Harbour, n.d.*

Mary had a little lamb,
Its fleece was white as snow;
And everywhere that Mary went
The lamb was sure to go.

It followed her to school one day,
It was against the rule,
And made the children laugh and play
To see a lamb at school.

Mary, Mary, quite contrary,
How does your garden grow?
With silver bells and cockle-shells
And pretty maids all in a row.

Old King Cole was a merry old soul,
And a merry old soul was he;
He called for his pipe, he called for his glass,
And he called for his fiddlers three.

Old Mother Hubbard
Went to the cupboard
To fetch her poor dog a bone;
But when she came there
The cupboard was bare,
And so the poor dog had none.

She went to the barber's
To buy him a wig,
But when she came back
He was dancing a jig.

Pat-a-cake, pat-a-cake, baker's man.
So I will, Master, as fast as I can.
Pat it, and prick it, and mark it with B,
Put it in the oven for baby and me.

Peter, Peter, pumpkin eater,
Had a wife, and couldn't keep her;
He put her in a pumpkin shell,
And there he kept her very well.

Peter Piper picked a peck
Of pickled pepper;
A peck of pickled pepper
Peter Piper picked.

Polly put the kettle on,
Polly put the kettle on,
Polly put the kettle on,
We'll all have tea.

Sukey take it off again,
Sukey take it off again,
Sukey take it off again,
They've all gone away.

Rain, rain, go away;
Come again another day;
Little Suzy wants to play.

Ring-a-ring of roses,
A pocket full of posies.
Tishoo! Tishoo!
We all fall down.

Rub a dub dub,
Three men in a tub;
And who do you think they be?
The butcher, the baker,
The candlestick maker;
Turn 'em out, knaves all three!

See, saw, Margery Daw,
Johnny shall have a new master;
He shall have but a penny a day,
Because he can't work any faster.

Simple Simon met a pie man,
Going to the fair;
Says Simple Simon to the pie man,
"Let me taste your ware."

Says the pie man unto Simon,
"First give me a penny."
Says Simple Simon to the pie man,
"I have not got any."

Simple Simon went a-fishing
For to catch a whale;
And all the water he had got
Was in his mother's pail.

Sing a song of sixpence,
A pocket full of rye;
Four-and-twenty blackbirds
Baked in a pie.

When the pie was opened,
The birds began to sing;
Was not that a dainty dish
To set before the king?

The lion and the unicorn
Were fighting for the crown;
The lion beat the unicorn
All round about the town.

Some gave them white bread,
And some gave them brown;
Some gave them plum-cake,
And sent them out of town.

The man in the moon
Came down too soon
To inquire the way to Norwich;
The man in the south,
He burnt his mouth
With eating cold plum porridge.

The queen of hearts,
She made some tarts,
All on a summer's day;
The knave of hearts,
He stole those tarts,
And took them clean away.

Three little kittens
They lost their mittens,
And they began to cry,
Oh, mother dear, we sadly fear
Our mittens we have lost.

What! lost your mittens,
You naughty kittens!
Then you shall have no pie.
Mee-ow, mee-ow, mee-ow.
No, you shall have no pie.

The three little kittens
They found their mittens,
And they began to cry,
Oh, mother dear, see here, see here,
Our mittens we have found.

Put on your mittens,
You silly kittens,
And you shall have some pie.
Purr-r, purr-r, purr-r,
Oh, let us have some pie.

There was a crooked man, and he went a crooked mile,
He found a crooked sixpence against a crooked stile,
He bought a crooked cat, which caught a crooked mouse,
And they all lived together in a crooked little house.

There was an old woman who lived in a shoe;
She had so many children she didn't know what to do.
She gave them some broth without any bread;
Then whipped them all soundly and put them to bed.

This little pig went to market;
This little pig stayed home;
This little pig had roast beef;
This little pig had none;
This little pig cried "Wee, wee, wee!"
All the way home.

Three blind mice, see how they run!
They all ran after the farmer's wife,
Who cut off their tails with a carving knife,
Did you ever see such a thing in your life,
As three blind mice?

Tom, Tom, the piper's son,
Learned to play when he was young,
But all the tunes that he could play,
Was "Over the Hills and Far Away"!

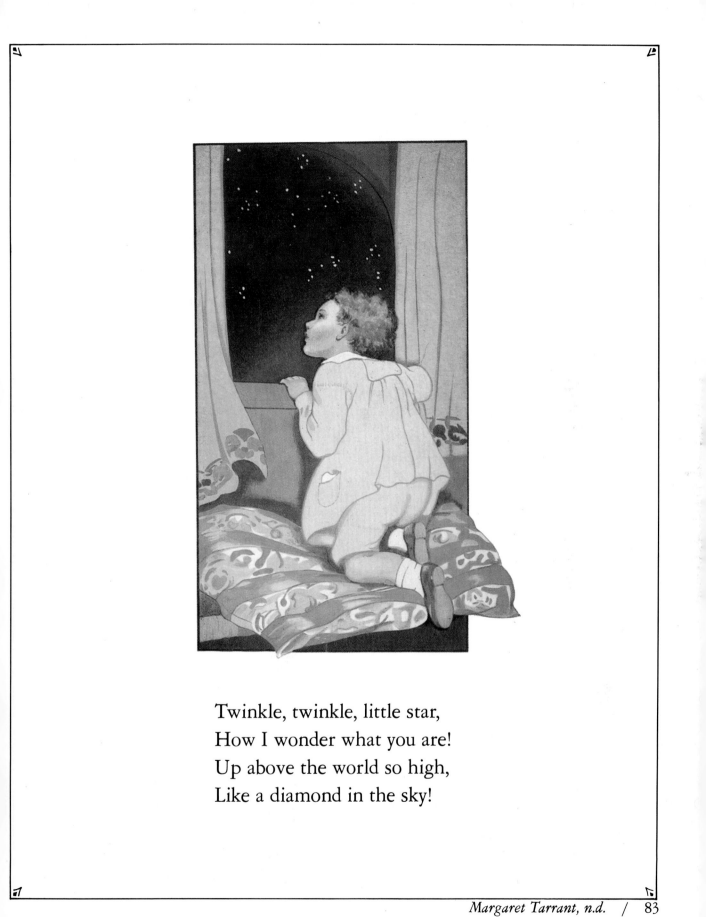

Twinkle, twinkle, little star,
How I wonder what you are!
Up above the world so high,
Like a diamond in the sky!

Wee Willie Winkie runs through the town,
Upstairs and downstairs in his nightgown,
Tapping at the window, crying through the lock,
"Are the babes in their beds,
For it's now ten o'clock?"

Acknowledgments

For the use of illustrations in this book that are covered by copyrights, I thank the following. Illustrations by Fanny V. Cory from *The Fanny Cory Mother Goose*, copyright 1913, 1917, and renewed 1941, 1945, by Macmillan Publishing Company. Used by permission of Macmillan Publishing Company. Illustrations by E. Boyd Smith reprinted by permission of G. P. Putnam's Sons from *The Boyd Smith Mother Goose*, copyright 1919 by G. P. Putnam's Sons, copyright renewed 1946 by Mary E. McD Smith. Illustrations by Jessie Willcox Smith from *The Little Mother Goose*, published by Dodd, Mead and Company, and used with their permission. An illustration by Milo Winter for *Alice's Adventures in Wonderland*, copyright 1916 by Rand McNally and Company is used by permission of Macmillan Publishing Company. Illustrations by Anne Anderson from *Old Mother Goose* are reprinted with the permission of the original publisher, Thomas Nelson. Illustrations by Marjory Hood from *Nursery Rhymes and Proverbs* are used with the permission of Eyre and Spottiswoode, the original publisher. Frederick Richardson's pictures from *Mother Goose, The Volland Edition*, published by P. F. Volland and Co., are used with the permission of Macmillan Publishing Company. Arthur Rackham's pictures from *Mother Goose, The Old Nursery Rhymes* are reprinted by permission of William Heinemann Limited. Mary Royt's illustrations from *Mother Goose, Her Own Book*, originally published by Reilly and Lee, and copyrighted in 1932 by E.M. Kovar, are used with the permission of Macmillan Publishing Company. For the use of pictures by Charles Robinson and John Hassall from *Mother Goose's Book of Nursery Stories, Rhymes, and Fables* we have the permission of the original publisher, Blackie and Son Limited. If inadvertently any other copyrighted material has been included in this volume, I offer my apologies and the willingness to correct the situation in future printings.

THE
END . .